# The Wheels on the Bus

*To Alice Kovalski*

Published by The Trumpet Club
1540 Broadway, New York, New York 10036

ISBN: 0-440-84409-6

This edition published by arrangement with Joy Street/Little, Brown and Company (Inc.)

Musical notation by Miriam Katzin

Printed in the United States of America
September 1991

10 9 8 7 6
UPC

# Maryann Kovalski

# The Wheels on the Bus

A TRUMPET CLUB SPECIAL EDITION

One day, Grandma took Jenny and Joanna shopping for new winter coats.

They tried on long coats and short coats,
blue coats and red coats, plaid coats and even
raincoats. Joanna chose a coat with wooden
barrel buttons. Jenny liked it too,
because of the hood.

When it was time to go home, the bus didn't come for a long time and everyone grew tired. "I have an idea, sweeties," said Grandma. "Let's sing a song my Granny sang with me when I was a little girl." And so they began to sing. . . .

The wipers on the bus go swish, swish, swish

swish, swish, swish

swish, swish, swish

The wipers on the bus go swish, swish, swish

all around the town.

The people on the bus hop on and off

on and off

on and off

The people on the bus hop on and off

all around the town.

The horn on the bus goes toot, toot, toot

    toot, toot, toot

    toot, toot, toot

The horn on the bus goes toot, toot, toot

    all around the town.

The money on the bus goes clink, clink, clink

clink, clink, clink

clink, clink, clink

The money on the bus goes clink, clink, clink

all around the town.

The people on the bus go up and down

up and down

up and down

The people on the bus go up and down

all around the town.

The babies on the bus go waaa, waaa, waaa

    waaa, waaa, waaa

    waaa, waaa, waaa

The babies on the bus go waaa, waaa, waaa

    all around the town.

The parents on the bus go ssh, ssh, ssh

ssh, ssh, ssh

ssh, ssh, ssh

The parents on the bus go ssh, ssh, ssh

all around the town.

The wheels on the bus go round and round

round and round

round and round

The wheels on the bus go round and round

all around the town.

Grandma, Jenny, and Joanna had so much fun . . .

They missed the bus!

So . . .

They took a taxi.